The Tiara Club

For Princess Jenny and
her lovely mum too, xxx
VF

For mum and dad,
with love,
SG

www.tiaraclub.co.uk

ORCHARD BOOKS
338 Euston Road, London NW1 3BH
Orchard Books Australia
Hachette Children's Books
Level 17/207 Kent Street, Sydney, NSW 2000, Australia
A Paperback Original
First published in Great Britain in 2005
Text © copyright Vivian French 2005
Illustrations © copyright Sarah Gibb 2005
The rights of Vivian French and Sarah Gibb to be
identified as the author and illustrator of this work
have been asserted by them in accordance with
the Copyright, Designs and Patents Act, 1988.

A CIP catalogue record for this book is available
from the British Library.
ISBN 1 84362 862 7
5 7 9 10 8 6 4

Printed in Great Britain

The Tiara Club

Princess Sophia
and the Sparkling Surprise

By Vivian French
Illustrated by Sarah Gibb

ORCHARD BOOKS

The Royal Palace Academy
for the Preparation of Perfect Princesses

(Known to our students as 'The Princess Academy')

OUR SCHOOL MOTTO:
*A Perfect Princess always thinks of others before herself,
and is kind, caring and truthful.*

We offer the complete curriculum for all princesses, including –

How to talk to a Dragon	*Designing and Creating the Perfect Ball Gown*
Creative Cooking for Perfect Palace Parties	*Avoiding Magical Mistakes*
Wishes, and how to use them Wisely	*Descending a Staircase as if Floating on Air*

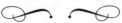

Our head teacher, Queen Gloriana, is present at all times, and students are well looked after by the school Fairy Godmother.

Visiting tutors and experts include –

KING PERCIVAL (Dragons)	*QUEEN MOTHER MATILDA (Etiquette, Posture and Poise)*
LADY VICTORIA (Banquets)	*THE GRAND HIGH DUCHESS DELIA (Costume)*

We award tiara points to encourage
our princesses towards the next level.
All princesses who win enough points in their
first year are welcomed to the Tiara Club
and presented with a silver tiara.

Tiara Club princesses are invited to return
next year to Silver Towers, our very special
residence for Perfect Princesses, where
they may continue their education
at a higher level.

PLEASE NOTE:
Princesses are expected to arrive at the Academy
with a *minimum* of:

TWENTY BALL GOWNS
*(with all necessary hoops,
petticoats, etc)*

TWELVE DAY DRESSES

SEVEN GOWNS
*suitable for garden parties,
and other special
day occasions*

TWELVE TIARAS

DANCING SHOES
five pairs

VELVET SLIPPERS
three pairs

RIDING BOOTS
two pairs

*Cloaks, muffs, stoles, gloves
and other essential
accessories as required*

Hello! My name is Princess Sophia, and I'm SO pleased you're keeping us company here at the Princess Academy. Have you met the others from Rose Room? There's Alice, and Katie, and Daisy and Charlotte and Emily, and we've been best friends ever since we met on the very first day of term. We all look after each other. Which is a Very Good Thing when there are princesses like Perfecta around. She's so MEAN! Alice's big sister says Perfecta got hardly ANY tiara points in her first year at the Academy, and Queen Gloriana (that's our head teacher) wouldn't let her join the fabulous Tiara Club. She had to repeat a year, so she's here with us, and that means TROUBLE!

Chapter One

We were just finishing breakfast, and Charlotte was saying how BORING it was because there were no balls or parties to look forward to, when suddenly Fairy G appeared from nowhere in a cloud of silver sparkles. (Fairy G is the school fairy godmother, and she's quite AMAZINGLY big.)

Fairy G dusted away the sparkles, and beamed at us.

"I've got a VERY special treat for you first years," she said.

"Queen Gloriana has cancelled your usual lessons, and you're to spend ALL DAY in the sewing room with the Grand High Duchess Delia!" And she looked as if she was expecting a MASSIVE cheer...but there wasn't one.

Nobody said anything, until Perfecta put up her hand.

"Excuse me, Fairy G," she said, "but you aren't expecting us to do any SEWING, are you?" She made it sound like the worst thing you could ever ever do – worse than picking up worms!

Fairy G gave Perfecta a chilly look. "Of COURSE I am, Perfecta," she said. "The Grand High Duchess is the best needlewoman in the whole kingdom! Her designs for ballgowns and dresses are TRULY wonderful, and you're very VERY lucky she's agreed to spend a day here."

Perfecta made a dreadful face. "My mother and father would be FURIOUS if they thought I was making my own dresses," she sneered. "That's for servants to do!"

I held my breath and waited for

Fairy G to explode, but she didn't. Well, not quite. "I would like to remind you, Princess Perfecta," she said, and she sounded terribly stern, "that tiara points are won AND lost in many different ways. Be VERY careful!" She turned to the rest of us. "Hurry up, now! Duchess Delia is waiting for you. Make sure you wash your hands before you make your way to the sewing room – and I'm sure we'll ALL have a lovely day!" And she disappeared, but this time in the usual way through the dining room door.

As soon as she was gone we all started talking at once.

"I'm HOPELESS at sewing," Katie wailed. "I tried to make a dress for one of my dolls once, and it was AWFUL!"

"Me too," Charlotte agreed. "I always sew the wrong bits to each other!"

"AND me," said Emily.

"And I ALWAYS prick my fingers," Daisy said.

"It might be OK," Alice said cheerfully. "Gran makes quite a lot of my clothes, and I help her sometimes. It's fun – we think of all kinds of ways we can use old velvet curtains, or the left over bits of satin from Granpapa's royal sashes."

"OLD VELVET CURTAINS?" Perfecta and her horrible friend, Princess Floreen, were standing right beside Alice, and staring at her in the MOST despising way.

Alice giggled. "Yes! One of my most favourite winter ballgowns was made of HEAVENLY red velvet from the throne room!"

Perfecta put her arm round Floreen's shoulder. "If you ask ME, Floreen," she said with a sniff, "princesses who are so POOR that they have to make their dresses from CURTAINS shouldn't be allowed to come to the Academy! I mean, we might just as well invite in BEGGARS and TRAMPS!

"PROPER Princesses are RICH, AND they have servants. How on EARTH can you join the Tiara Club if you haven't even got a SEWING MAID?" And she tossed her head, and was just about to march away when I grabbed Alice and swept her past Perfecta and out into the middle of the dining hall.

Chapter Two

I do know it is NOT being a
Perfect Princess to go round
grabbing people. I really do! But
Perfecta made me so MAD I
couldn't help it. For a second
I didn't care one bit about tiara
points, or even the Tiara Club.
I held Alice's hand, and I said
in my VERY loudest voice,

"Sometimes Princess Perfecta is SO STUPID! The richest princess in the whole wide world would NEVER be as special as YOU are, Alice! Being a Perfect Princess is NOTHING to do with money –

it's all about being kind, and truthful, and looking after other people, and thinking about other people before yourself – but I don't think princesses like Perfecta and Floreen will EVER be clever enough to understand such things!" And then I whirled Alice out of the dining hall and into the corridor outside.

"WOW!" Alice said. "That told her! And right in front of everybody, too!"

I leant against the wall, and tried to look calm and graceful, the way a Perfect Princess should, but my heart was beating really fast.

"She deserved it," I said. "How COULD she say that? She's SUCH a snob!"

Alice gave me a hug. "Thank you SO much for standing up for me! But do you know what? I don't care what she thinks – I don't think she's worth

bothering about." She peered back into the dining hall. "Here come the rest of Rose Room!"

Alice was right. Charlotte and the others came hurrying out of the dining hall to join us.

"What's Perfecta doing?" Alice wanted to know.

"She's absolutely FURIOUS," Charlotte said. "She and Floreen are muttering together – they're probably planning a dreadful revenge!"

I'd calmed down a bit, and part of me was beginning to worry. It wasn't Perfect OR Princessy to call someone stupid in front of EVERYONE in the first year...but, I told myself, Perfecta HAD been truly horrible to Alice. We went off to the cloakroom to wash our hands, and as we were coming out again I saw Perfecta and Floreen walking towards me.

All at once a sort of fight broke

out inside my head. Have you ever had that happen? Part of me wanted to walk right past Perfecta and pretend she wasn't there, but another bit of me was telling me I should smile at her as if nothing had happened, and ANOTHER bit was wondering if I should say sorry.

I didn't have to decide. Perfecta came straight up to me.

"Do you know what YOU are, Princess Sophia?" she hissed. "You're a horrible GOODY GOODY! You're SO sugary sweet and nice-as-pie you make me SICK! But don't think you can get away with it!

Just because you've got mimsy-
wimsy yellow curls, and you're
one of the silly old dozy rosie-
posies, that doesn't mean you
can pick on me in front of
everybody! You're a horrible la-
di-da SHOW OFF!" And then
she STORMED into the
cloakroom, slamming the door
so loudly that bits of plaster
fell off the ceiling. Floreen
scuttled after her, and as she
vanished she squeaked, "And
we're going to get you back – so
THERE!"

"Oh dear," I said.

"Just ignore her," Alice said.

27

"Come on! Let's go and see what this Grand High Duchess has lined up for us!"

"She'd never dare do anything anyway," Daisy said. "Whatever would Queen Gloriana and Fairy G say if they found one princess sticking pins into another?"

That made me laugh, and we bounced into the sewing room to find Duchess Delia and Fairy G arranging HUGE piles of GORGEOUS material on the tables...and when I say gorgeous, I really REALLY mean it. I'd never seen anything like it in my whole life. There were smooth plushy velvets, and the softest fluffiest wool, and rolls and rolls of crunchy petticoat lace...and they were ALL as white as the cleanest crispiest snow! It looked utterly utterly MAGIC.

"DO come in, my dears," Duchess Delia said, and she pointed to an empty table. Most of the rest of our year were already sitting at the other tables whispering to each other, and I just KNEW they were talking about my quarrel with Perfecta. Then the sewing room door opened again, and the whispering stopped dead, so I knew Perfecta had come in – and do you know what? I felt SO uncomfortable I nearly burst into tears.

Chapter Three

I think Fairy G MUST have known that something was going on, because she always does...but she deals with things in her own way. Even so, I was SHOCKED when she made Perfecta and Floreen sit with us at our table. I waited for Perfecta to say something, and she did – but not

AT ALL what I'd expected. She made sure Duchess Delia was looking, and then she said in a sweet-little-girly voice, "Oh, Alice! How LOVELY! You know ALL about sewing, don't you? I'm HONOURED to sit next to you!"

Alice didn't know WHAT to do! She gave a sort of gasp.

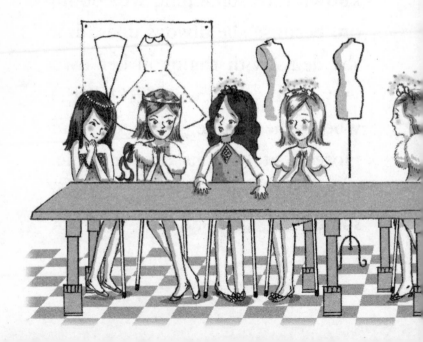

"Ooof – er...thank you!"

Fairy G gave Perfecta SUCH an odd look. Then she beamed at the rest of us. "Now, let's give our special guest an ENORMOUS Princess Academy welcome!"

And we all clapped – although I was SO wondering what Perfecta was up to.

Duchess Delia peered at us over her spectacles, and Fairy G coughed. "Ahem. Perhaps you'd like to tell the princesses about their task for today, Duchess?"

The Duchess nodded. "Oh, I would! Now, girls – it's such FUN! You're each going to design and make your very own winter ballgown, and you'll wear it to the Princess Academy Surprise—"

"HARRRRRUMPH!!!"

She was interrupted by a MASSIVE roar from Fairy G, but it was too late. We were all sitting bolt upright, our eyes shining. A SURPRISE???

Katie put up her hand.

"Please – dear DEAR Fairy G – WHAT surprise?"

Fairy G folded her arms. "You'll just have to wait and see!" she said firmly. "It won't BE a surprise if we tell you!"

Duchess Delia positively giggled. "Oh dearie me," she said, "I'm so sorry! But now, girls – here are a few of my winter designs to give you some ideas. I've asked some of the Tiara Club Princesses to model for me..." And she clapped her hands...and we GASPED!

A line of BEAUTIFUL princesses came sweeping in through the sewing room door, wearing the most GLORIOUS dresses you've EVER seen. Our eyes opened as wide as saucers! Normally we never see any of the Tiara Club Princesses because they stay in

the Silver Towers on the other
side of the valley, and they don't
have anything to do with us.

Alice's big sister is there, and Alice only EVER sees her in the holidays. Each princess sailed into the middle of the room, twirled three times, and then posed for a moment before twirling once more.

Alice suddenly gave a loud

squeak. "Look!" she whispered. "That's my big sis!!!" And a dark haired princess (she looked SO like Alice!) did an extra twirl RIGHT in front of us, and winked a tiny wink as she swirled off through the door.

As the last one swept away I found I was holding my breath – they were SO gorgeous. And they made me feel SO odd...

Maybe I should tell you something. A secret. PLEASE don't tell.

Ever since I was tiny I've ALWAYS wanted to be a Perfect Princess and to join the Tiara Club. I really DO try to be kind and helpful, not because I want to be a goody-goody, but because it's what princesses do. Seeing the Tiara Club Princesses made me remember that I'd SHOUTED at

Perfecta...and it made me feel as if I was total failure. How would I EVER get to join the Tiara Club if I behaved like that? And I made myself a promise to try MUCH HARDER.

The Duchess positively glowed, she was so pleased we liked her dresses. "And now it's YOUR turn," she said. "Just remember that every SPECK of dirt will show on the white, so DO be careful." And she handed each of us a piece of paper, a pencil, a packet of needles and thread and a MASSIVE pair of scissors!

I nearly had a fit when Duchess Delia gave me those scissors. I could just imagine HUGE piles of ruined velvet, and me with NOTHING to wear...but I'd forgotten that Fairy G had magic powers. It was FANTASTIC!!! We each drew

our ideal dress (Duchess Delia came round and helped us) and then Fairy G tapped the material we'd chosen with her wand, and IMMEDIATELY the scissors zoomed off ALL ON THEIR OWN and cut the PERFECT shape!!!! And then

the needles sewed it up with such TEENY stitches you could hardly see them. And the best bit was that if something looked wrong, you just rubbed out your picture, and drew your dress a different way, and – TINGLE ZINGLE!!! The scissors and the needles sorted it out!!!

Chapter Four

By the time the lunch bell went we were all positively fizzing with excitement. The sewing room tables were HEAPED with beautiful dresses, and hoops and petticoats and sashes...but one thing was REALLY weird.

Perfecta was behaving as if she was the most amazingly

PERFECT Princess ever! When I dropped my needle she totally LEAPT to pick it up – AND she threaded it for me! And she KEPT saying how fabulous my dress was.

Of course, Duchess Delia thought Perfecta was WONDERFUL.

"SUCH a kind, thoughtful, generous girl," she said. "I shall give you TWENTY tiara points right now!"

Perfecta curtsied very low...but as she got up again I'm ALMOST sure I saw her wink at Floreen.

We finally managed to get away from Perfecta in the lunch queue, and Charlotte immediately said, "WHAT'S GOING ON?"

"She's up to something," Katie said darkly. "She was winking at Floreen."

"I suppose she MIGHT have decided to try and be good,"

Daisy said. "After all, Fairy G did give her a huge warning at breakfast."

"But that was before she had a go at me and Sophia," Alice pointed out.

Emily rubbed her nose. "It's VERY odd. Hey, what do you think the Surprise is?"

"I think it's some kind of outdoors party," Alice said. "That white velvet's REALLY thick!"

"But it's not cold outside," Daisy said. "The sun's shining!"

"I suppose we'll have to wait and see," Emily sighed. "Maybe Fairy G'll tell us after lunch."

But Fairy G didn't. She said she had Important Business to see to, and she'd see us later.

We spent the afternoon decorating our dresses. Duchess Delia had brought in baskets of rainbow coloured beads and feathers and ribbons (they looked FABULOUS on the white dresses!)

and bunches of heavenly little silk
roses in all kinds of pastel colours.
And Perfecta went on being
AMAZINGLY perfect. She MADE
me take the one and only bunch
of pink silk roses, and I know
she wanted them really badly for
herself because she absolutely
SNATCHED them out of the
basket! She even helped me pin
them onto the front of my dress.

"There!" she said. "Don't they
look GORGEOUS?"

They did, and I thanked
Perfecta as enthusiastically as
I could, but my brain was doing
somersaults.

Could Daisy possibly be right?
Was Princess Perfecta really and
TRULY trying to be good?

"LOOK! It's SNOWING!!!"

Princess Freya was waving her
arms in excitement, and I forgot
all about Perfecta as I dashed to
the windows to look.

Freya was right. Huge white snowflakes were tumbling from the sky, and the academy was looking like a magical fairy palace.

"But it's the wrong time of year!" Princess Lisa said. "It

CAN'T snow now!"

Duchess Delia laughed. "It can do whatever Fairy G tells it to do, dear! Have you seen the lake?"

We stared and stared. The lake had frozen into a sparkling silver mirror...

"OH!" Alice clapped her hands. "A SKATING PARTY!"

"EXACTLY, my dear," Duchess Delia said. "A Sparkling Ice Extravaganza! Now, all of you finish your dresses, and hang them on the rail. You're to go downstairs for an early supper, and then come back to change and get ready. As you go outside you will each be given skating boots and a muff...and then all that is left will be for you to enjoy yourselves!"

Chapter Five

I was the last to leave the sewing room. Everyone else tumbled out in a chattering rush, but I waited behind. I'd made a decision...

Duchess Delia asked me what was wrong.

"Please," I said, and I curtsied. "I'd like to surprise Princess Perfecta. I was horrid to her this

55

morning...so would it be all right if I let her have the pink silk roses for her dress? I know she'd like them."

"What a SWEET girl you are!" Duchess Delia cooed. "Just the PERFECT friend for dear Perfecta! Of COURSE you may put the roses on her dress...here, let me help you." And she whipped out a needle and thread and stitched the roses onto Perfecta's dress, just the way they'd been on mine.

"Perfect for Perfecta," she smiled. "And I know she LOVED your dress, Sophia dear, so let's just give hers a couple of extra little tweaks, shall we?" And she pinned and tucked and stitched, and in two minutes Perfecta's dress was frilled and gathered and looped EXACTLY like mine.

"THERE!" said Duchess Delia.

"The dear girl was so busy looking after you and your friends that she never took time to think about herself. She'll have SUCH a lovely surprise!" And she wafted away down the stairs, and I went down to the dining hall.

Of course all of Rose Room wanted to know what I'd been doing.

"Honestly," Charlotte said when I told her. "You're just TOO nice, Sophia. Why should Perfecta have the roses AND the prettiest dress? She's only been good for one day!"

"She's up to something," Katie added.

"She was HORRIBLE at breakfast," Emily said. "WHY are you being so nice to her?"

I shuffled my feet. "You'll think I'm stupid."

Alice shook her head. "No we won't."

"We're your FRIENDS!" Daisy said.

"Well," I said slowly. "I kept thinking about what I said at breakfast. About PERFECT princesses thinking about others before themselves. And being kind. Even if Perfecta WAS horrible, that didn't mean I had to be horrible back."

When supper was over we went back to the sewing room, which was full of giggling first years sitting at the tables. Fairy G and Duchess Delia were already looking WONDERFULLY grand as they stood in front of the rail of beautiful winter ballgowns.

"What's up with Perfecta?" Charlotte whispered in my ear. "Does she know about her dress?"

Perfecta did look very pink, and her eyes were gleaming.

"I don't think so," I said – and at that moment Fairy G held up the first dress.

"One TRULY beautiful dress decorated with pink silk roses! Tell me, who does this belong to?"

I put up my hand. "Please, Fairy G, that belongs to Princess Perfecta!" I took an extra deep breath. "And I'd like to say I'm sorry I was horrid this morning, and I hope she'll forgive me!"

There was a tiny amazed silence – and then Perfecta leapt to her feet.

"No – it's not! It's NOT my dress! It's SOPHIA's!"

Duchess Delia smiled a massive smile. "Aha! But that's where you're wrong, Perfecta dear! Look! Sophia and I have put the pink roses on YOUR dress as a surprise!! THIS is

Sophia's dress—" She picked the next dress off the rail, and lifted it up – and we GASPED.

There was a huge black stain right the way down the front. It looked DREADFUL!!!

Nobody said anything. We were MUCH too shocked. Fairy G looked grim, and picked up the next dress – and that was covered in ink as well. And the next. AND the next...in fact, the one and only dress without a mark on it was Perfecta's.

"Princess Perfecta," Fairy G

said, and she looked at Perfecta in SUCH a meaningful way. "Can you explain why the only dress without any ink is yours?"

Perfecta's face went a horrible green colour, and she positively SHRIEKED, "But it's NOT my dress! It IS Sophia's! ISN'T IT, Floreen?"

Floreen nodded. "Yes. And it proves she's guilty! She spoiled all the other dresses, but she wouldn't spoil her own—"

Fairy G stared at Floreen. Then she asked in a TOTALLY scary voice, "And WHY should Princess Sophia want to spoil everyone else's dresses, Princess Floreen?"

"Because she's a show-off," Floreen said indignantly. "She thinks she's the best at EVERYTHING. Perfecta said it would serve her jolly well right if everyone hated HER for a change, instead of..." Her voice died away, and she went BRIGHT red.

You can just IMAGINE the noise. Everybody was talking at once, and Fairy G had to swell up to her LARGEST size and BELLOW before we were quiet.

"RIGHT!" she boomed.

"Princess Perfecta and Princess Floreen! STRAIGHT TO QUEEN GLORIANA'S STUDY!!!" And she hooshed the two miserable princesses out...but then she stopped, and beamed her enormous grin.

"Ooops!" she said. "I nearly forgot!" She waved her wand...and AT ONCE every single ink stain VANISHED!!!

"THERE!" she said. "BETTER than new!"

Duchess Delia shook her head. "I'm shocked," she said, "really shocked. But now, let's see how you look in your gowns!"

Chapter Six

The Sparkling Ice Extravaganza
was SO LOVELY!!! Tiny icicle
lights twinkled on every tree, and
the silver frozen lake reflected the
millions of stars shining in the dark
blue sky. Our ice skating boots
were snow white like our dresses,
and our muffs were the SOFTEST
white fur (not real, of course!)

sprinkled with shimmering pearls. A wonderful orchestra was already playing on a silver bandstand, and a full moon shone above them. The music was GLORIOUS! We spun and we twirled, and when it came to

the polka we fairly FLEW over the ice! And then our Head Teacher, Queen Gloriana, came gliding out like a beautiful swan. She sailed into the middle of us, and the music stopped as she held up her hand.

"I don't want to keep you from your fun," she told us, "but I have a special award to make. Early today Princess Sophia was carried away by her desire to protect a friend from an unkind attack which, I regret to say, came from two other princesses here at the Academy. Like any true princess Sophia realised her mistake, and did her best to set things right with a gift and an apology...but sadly the two princesses had already decided to take an unpleasant revenge on Sophia for her outspoken opinion. THAT matter is now being dealt with,

but I would very much like to recognise, here at the Sparkling Ice Extravaganza, Princess Sophia's most EXCELLENT example of How to be a Perfect Princess – and I hereby award

her FIFTY tiara points! And now, music PLEASE!" And Queen Gloriana gave me a dazzling smile, and as I sank into my deepest curtsey she sailed away across the ice...and do you know what?

I felt exactly as if I was sparkling inside AND out, and as Alice and Charlotte and Emily and Daisy and Katie and I held hands to swing round and round I really did believe that one day – ONE DAY! – I'd be a Perfect Princess and win my place in the Tiara Club...and you'll be there too. I just KNOW you will!

What happens next?
Find out in

Princess Emily
and the Beautiful Fairy

Hi there! I'm Princess Emily — one of
the Rose Room princesses at the
Princess Academy. Do you know Alice and
Katie and Daisy and Charlotte and Sophia?
They're my best friends — just like you!
And have you met Princess Perfecta yet?
She's HORRID. Alice says it's because
Queen Gloriana (our head teacher) made
her repeat her first year — she didn't
get enough tiara points to get
into the Tiara Club!
Ooooh...just thinking about it
makes me shivery. It would be so
DREADFUL to have to start all over
again. Can you IMAGINE it?
Oh nooooooo!

Check out

The
Tiara
Club

website at:

www.tiaraclub.co.uk

You'll find Perfect Princess games and fun things to do, as well as news on the Tiara Club and all your favourite princesses!

Win a Tiara Club
Perfect Princess Prize!

Look for the secret word in mirror writing hidden in
a tiara in each of the Tiara Club books. Each book
has one word. Put together the six words from books
1 to 6 to make a special Perfect Princess sentence,
then send it to us. Each month, we will put the
correct entries in a draw and one lucky reader will
receive a magical Perfect Princess prize!

Send your Perfect Princess sentence, your name
and your address on a postcard to:
THE TIARA CLUB COMPETITION,
Orchard Books, 338 Euston Road,
London, NW1 3BH

Australian readers should write to:
Hachette Children's Books,
Level 17/207 Kent Street, Sydney, NSW 2000.

Only one entry per child.
Final draw: 31 October 2006

The Tiara Club

By Vivian French
Illustrated by Sarah Gibb

All priced at £3.99.

The Tiara Club books are available from all good bookshops,
or can be ordered direct from the publisher:
Orchard Books, PO BOX 29, Douglas IM99 1BQ.
Credit card orders please telephone 01624 836000 or fax 01624 837033
or visit our Internet site: www.wattspub.co.uk
or e-mail: bookshop@enterprise.net for details.

To order please quote title, author, ISBN and your full name and address.
Cheques and postal orders should be made payable to 'Bookpost plc.'
Postage and packing is FREE within the UK
(overseas customers should add £2.00 per book).

Prices and availability are subject to change.